Robbers in the Town

*The gang of six – and Patchie – are
back on the beat, hoping to make a few bob
in the big gardens of the nobs up on
the North Circular Road.
But they soon realize that a real life drama
is unfolding next door.
What is the mystery surrounding gentle
Linda and her grandfather?
Is the grim-faced Mrs. Coffey hatching a
plot? And what part does the sinister figure
they call 'the dancer' play . . . ?
The gang take a hand in a fast-moving story
of intrigue and suspense.*

Carolyn Swift

Robbers in the Town

Illustrated by Terry Myler

ACORN BOOKS
The Children's Press

To Deirdre
who is the dancer in our family,
though not at all like the one
in this book

First published in 1983 by
The Children's Press Limited
90 Lower Baggot Street, Dublin 2

© Text Carolyn Swift
© Illustrations The Children's Press

This book is published with the assistance of the
Arts Council (An Chomhairle Ealaíon), Dublin.
The author was assisted by a contribution from
the Author's Royalty Scheme of the Arts Council

ISBN 0 900068 74 4 cased
ISBN 0 90068 68 X paper

Typesetting by Computertype Limited
Printed in Ireland by Mount Salus Press Limited

Contents

Up and down the houses,
  Each shall have a share;
In and out the windows,
  Steady on the stair;
Round and round the garden,
  Like a dancing Bear;
One step, two steps,
  And tickly under there

1 Up and Down the Houses

May Byrne jumped out of bed and ran to look out of the window of the little yellow-brick house below the dome of the Four Courts, beside the River Liffey. Sunlight was already filling the Square, lighting up the end wall where once she had spent most of her free time playing Plainy-Clappy with her friends Maura and Imelda. She was older now and, with the long summer holidays stretching ahead of her, she had more ambitious plans.

With the bikes she and her friends had got as a reward for discovering the treasure of St. Mary's Abbey, there was so much they could do. They could go out to Dollymount for a swim, or they could head off up the mountains to Ballinascorney to visit Larry Keogh and his wife on their farm — May knew the Keoghs would always have a welcome for her and her brother Richie and their friends, because of the help they had given them when the Blessington bank robbers had hidden there. As soon as she had helped to dress her youngest brother and had her breakfast, she ran across the Square to talk her plans over with Maura Reilly.

When Maura opened the door, May knew at once by the look on her face that something was wrong. She listened to what May had to say in glum silence.

Then she spoke almost sharply. 'It's all the one to me where you go,' she said, 'for I can't come anyways. Ma says I've to find work for the summer.'

'What sort of work?' asked May.

'I dunno. Cleanin', I suppose. Mammy doesn't care so long as I bring in the few bob.'

Maura's father had had no work for the past eighteen months and Maura's mother polished offices at night for the contract cleaners. Until now, she had been content so long as Maura earned a little every so often for baby-sitting, but now it seemed that this was not enough. It had been bound to happen, May thought. With everything always going up in price, no one ever had enough any more.

On her way back across the Square, she saw her elder brother Richie talking to Mickser Dolan from next door, and told them the news.

'That's funny,' said Richie. 'We were just talkin' about tryin' to make a few bob ourselves. Old Danny Noonan says he was drawin' his pay every week regular when he was our age.'

'He ran away to sea,' objected May, trying to picture her brother as a sailor. Would Richie too end up an old man, crippled with arthritis, bringing his chair outside his front door to sit in the sun in the Square and tell stories?

'I don't think it's that easy to get taken on as a cabin-boy these times,' she said doubtfully.

'I don't mean that, you gorm,' said Richie. 'Just something for the hollyers.'

'You mean, workin' in Flynn's, like Heno?' asked May, thinking of one of the lads from across the Square, who helped out for the holidays in a pub down on the Quays.

Richie shook his head. 'Mickser has a better idea.'

'If me Da can always get readies doin' gardens, why can't we?' Mickser pointed out.

Mickser's father worked as a boilerman with a firm of builders' providers, but May knew he did nixers at weekends as a gardener for the well-to-do up around the North Circular Road.

'But we've no tools,' she said.

'Nor had me Da when he started,' Mickser told her. 'The nobs with the big gardens all have sheds full of mowers and rakes and hedge-cutters, only they've no one to do the work for them anymore.'

'I was goin' to ask Whacker would he like to come too,' Richie said. Whacker was his closest pal and the brother of May's friend, Imelda.

'We could work as a team,' said Mickser. 'There's scads of gardens up there.'

Richie nodded. 'One could clip the hedges and another cut the grass and the third trim the borders. That way we could do a whole garden in a half-day and it would be more fun.'

Suddenly May had an idea. 'Why don't we all go?' she suggested. 'Then Maura wouldn't have to go out cleanin' on her own.'

'We could hardly have a whole clatter of us goin' around,' said Richie.

'There's more nor six doin' the contract cleanin' with Maura's mother,' May told him.

'They mightn't pay enough to be worth it for six,' objected Mickser.

'Wouldn't it be all the same in the end?' asked May. 'We'd do each garden quicker and so we could do more gardens. You said there were scads of them.'

'Let's ask Danny what he thinks,' said Richie, so they all three ran across the Square to where old Danny Noonan sat in front of his little front door, reading one of the hard-backed books he got every week from the Public Library.

'Well, well, and what can I do for you this fine morning?' he asked, putting a crumpled cigarette packet into the book to mark his place before he closed it.

'D'you think would we get work on the gardens along the North Circular, like Mickser's Da?' asked May. 'Enough for us and Maura and Whacker and Imelda too?'

Danny considered the matter, his blue eyes looking away into the distance as if he were looking through the walls of the houses all the way to the North Circular Road itself. Then he nodded.

'Why wouldn't you?' he said. 'For the North Circular runs all the ways from Summerhill right to the walls of the Phoenix Park.'

'Is that a long way?' May asked, for though she had been to the Park several times she had always

gone straight along the quays to the Parkgate Street entrance and did not know that way of going at all.

'Isn't it more than two miles long on a great big half circle', Danny told her. 'You see, long ago, when the city stretched for no more than a mile from where you are standing now, whichever way you faced, the North Circular was the northern boundary of the city, and the South Circular on the other side of the Liffey was the southern boundary. And ringing the city outside of them again were the two canals, the Royal Canal beyond the North Circular and the

11

Grand Canal beyond the South Circular, the two of them running out from either side of the mouth of the river down near the docks.'

'D'you mean that Ballyfermot wasn't in Dublin at all?' asked Richie in wonder, for his and May's Uncle Jack and Auntie Lil lived in Ballyfermot.

Danny laughed. 'That was all green fields even when I was a lad,' he said. 'But it was two hundred years ago that the North Circular was built to circle the city on the northern side, and three hundred years ago that the very first Duke of Ormonde planned a Royal Deer Park that was to become the Phoenix Park.'

'Three hundred years!' gasped May. 'Is it that old?'

Danny nodded. 'Of course, there was no zoo there then, only a spring of water so clear that even the fine ladies and gentlemen travelled in their carriages to drink it. That's what gave the Park it's name: Fionn Uisge. Only the English said it the best way they could manage and that sounded like Phoenix.'

'And did you learn all that from a book?' Richie asked, for sometimes it seemed to him as if there could be nothing in the whole world that Danny did not know.

Danny laughed. 'I did,' he said, 'and I learned that there were chancers in Dublin even in them times, and that even a duke could be conned.'

'How?' asked May, knowing that Danny needed only a little prod to start on one of his stories.

'Well, it was this way,' Danny began. 'The Duke of Ormonde asked a man be the name of Dodson to build the walls around his new park, so Dodson asked him for a whole load of money. Then didn't he go off to another lad and give him less than half of it to build the walls for him. And didn't he build them so badly that in only a few months they all fell down, and the deer ran out into the road and got all mixed up with the horses and carriages. And when the Duke asked Dodson what he had to say for himself, he had the cheek and impudence to say that if the Duke would only give him a hundred pounds every year he'd guarantee to keep the walls in good repair for his lifetime.'

'And were all the deer runnin' down the North Circular?' asked May.

Danny shook his head. 'No,' he said, 'for 'twasn't built then. But not long ago there were cows running down it near every day of the week.'

'Cows in Dublin!' May said in wonder.

'Indeed, and bullocks too,' Danny said, 'for the old Cattle Market was in the North Circular on the corner of Prussia Street. The whole space between the rows of big red-brick houses was filled with pens full of cattle, and there'd be buyers pokin' and proddin' them to see how much flesh they had on them. Many a time as a lad I'd watch them, biddin' and slappin' hands on the bargain. There'd be big buyers over from England, too, and then the drovers would herd cattle down the North Circular to the docks to load them on to the boat for Liverpool.'

'In amongst all the traffic?' asked Richie, trying to picture a cattle drive like in a Western on the telly, amidst all the cars and the lorries.

'Isn't that the very reason they moved the market,' Danny said. 'The traffic got too heavy, the same as it did with the Fruit and Vegetable Market beyond in St. Mary's Abbey. But it used to be a great sight, to see the young bullocks, scared stiff at the sight of the cars, all mooin' an' plungin' this way and that, and the big, red-necked drovers chasin' after them, cursin' an' swearin'.

'I'd love to have seen them,' said May. 'Did you help the drovers?'

'I did not,' said Danny, 'for I wasn't a local boy. But Brendan Behan, who lived off the North Circular in Russell Street, did.'

'Brendan Behan?' echoed Richie. 'D'you mean the man that wrote the plays?'

'The very same,' Danny told him. 'Many a time when he was a lad he'd make a few bob helping the cattle drovers on the North Circular Road.'

But by now Mickser was growing impatient. Danny's stories were all very well, he thought, but Richie and May would stay all day listening to them without really finding out what they wanted to know.

'And are there loads of rich people livin' in the big houses on the North Circular?' he asked.

'Well now, I wouldn't go so far as to say that!'

14

Danny conceded. 'They aren't quite as grand as they used to be and there's some of them now in flats. All the same, there's plenty of big houses still at the top end, runnin' up towards the Park. If I was you, I'd start from around Phibsboro' Church and work my way west.'

And that was how the six of them came to be heading off on their bikes up Church Street and Constitution Hill, bound for the North Circular Road.

Maura's mother had been against the idea at first. She was doubtful about how much money they would make, but she had finally been persuaded to let Maura try it for a week. If she did not bring home enough on the Friday, she would have to forget about it and go out cleaning.

When they had passed Phibsboro' Church and the shops, and crossed the bridge over the railway line, they got off their bikes and went into a huddle.

'We don't all want to go marchin' up to the door,' said Whacker. 'It'll scare them off. One or two's enough to get the job. Then we bring in the team.'

'Right,' said Richie. 'You and I'll go.'

'It was my idea,' Mickser complained.

'We can all try different houses,' said Whacker. 'It'll save time. We'll split up in twos. Richie and Maura, Mickser and Imelda, May and me.'

'Supposin' they all say "yes", what do we do?' asked Imelda, who did not see why her brother should suddenly be giving all the orders.

'They won't,' said Richie. 'Not all three of them. And if two of them do, we can do one this morning and one this evening.'

'Right,' said Whacker. 'May and me will take this first house here.' He pushed open the gate and set off up the pathway towards the steps, with May at his heels. Without waiting for him to ring the bell, the other four wheeled their bikes on up the road.

Richie and Maura tried the house next door. As they walked up the gravel sweep, Richie said, 'We oughta ask double for doin' this. Look at the state of the place.'

The hedges were ragged and the grass overgrown. Roses thrust their heads above a fine crop of dandelions, poppies and chickweed.

Maura looked nervously at the house. 'Maybe there's no one livin' here.' she said.

'There's curtains in the windows,' Richie pointed out.

'They could all be away.'

'We'll soon find out,' Richie said, boldly ringing the front door bell. It jangled discouragingly, an unmusical sound that echoed, as if through empty rooms. Nothing happened.

'I knew there'd be no one here,' said Maura.

Richie rang the bell again and knocked the big brass knocker that was dull for the want of polish.

Suddenly they heard a door slam and footsteps marching angrily across the hall. The door swung sharply open and a woman stood facing them. She had fair hair pulled severely back off her face in a bun, though she was 'younger than Mammy', thought Maura. She had mean little eyes in a flat featureless face, but what Maura noticed most about her were her hands. The palms were so large they made the thick fingers look almost stumpy, yet they gave a strange impression of power. Somehow Maura was sure she would not like to be at the mercy of those hands.

'Whatever ye are collectin' for, I've nothing for ye,' she snapped. Her voice was as hard and cold as her eyes. She started to close the door before she had even finished speaking, but Richie put out his foot to stop her.

'We're not collectin' for anything,' he said. 'We're doin' the gardens all up along, and we thought you might like yours done. It's badly in want of it.'

'That's no concern of yours,' she said sharply.

'We'd make a good job of it,' Richie told her, 'and leave all clean and tidy after us.'

'Ye'll be off about your business, or I'll get the Guards to ye,' she said, so fiercely that Richie took a step back and found himself facing a closed door.

'The mean ould divil!' he raged. 'Wouldn't you love to peg a few rocks in through her windows!'

Maura shivered. 'Let's get outa here,' she said. 'We don't wanna tangle with the likes of her. She'd give you the horrors.' Suddenly she grabbed Richie by the arm.

'Look!' she said.

Richie swung around from the door and saw they were not alone. Facing them from the far side of a laurel bush, across the tangled border, was a girl about their own age wearing dark glasses. Her hair was as red as Richie's but instead of being tousled and carrotty, it fell to her shoulders in a soft curtain of chestnut.

She was pretty, Maura thought, yet there was something about the fixed way she stood looking at them without speaking that seemed odd.

'Hullo,' she said. 'I didn't see you there.'

The girl smiled, almost as if she was reassured.

'I thought it might be the doctor,' she said.

'You can't be the full shilling if you think I look like a doctor,' said Richie.

The girl laughed.

'You certainly don't sound like him,' she said, and Maura thought that she had never met a girl who spoke with an accent like that though she had often heard it on television. It reminded her of the girl in *Black Beauty*.

'You're English, aren't you?' she asked.

The girl nodded. 'Yes,' she said. 'I'm sorry I thought your friend might be the doctor, but ... I can't see him.'

Richie shifted uncomfortably.

'You mean, you're blind?' he asked.

The girl nodded again.

'This is how I tell one person from another,' she said. She ran her soft fingers down over Richie's

18

freckled face and tip-tilted nose.

'I'm sorry,' Richie said, embarrassed. 'About saying you mustn't be the full shilling, I mean.'

'That's all right,' the girl said. 'Sighted people often don't realize at first. But I should have known it wasn't the doctor because he's always on his own and his step is much heavier than yours. It's just that I was expecting him.'

'Is someone sick then?' asked Maura.

'My grandfather,' said the girl. 'Of course, as soon as I heard Mrs. Coffey shouting at you, I knew it couldn't be the doctor.'

'Mrs. Coffey?' echoed Richie. 'Is that the name they put on old Sourpuss? One look from her would turn the milk and it straight from the dairy.'

Then he caught a glimpse of Whacker beyond the gate. 'We gotta go,' he said, moving off down the path.

Maura thought the girl looked disappointed. On impulse, she took the girl's hands and placed them on her own high cheekbones.

'My name's Maura and he's Richie,' she said. The girl lightly touched Maura's long nose, full lips and pointed chin.

'And I'm Linda,' she said. 'Will you be back this way again?'

'We're doin' the gardens,' Maura told her, 'but old Sourpuss didn't want this one done, though the dear knows it needs it.'

'She wouldn't,' said Linda with feeling, and

Maura guessed that she didn't like Mrs. Coffey any more than they did.

'Tell you what,' she said suddenly. 'When we've the gardens done we'll give you a shout, if you're still here.'

'Oh, I'll be here all right,' Linda said.

'See you, then,' said Maura, 'and I hope you've good news of your grand-da.' Then she ran off after Richie.

'Did yous have any luck?' asked Whacker, as Richie joined May and him at the gate.

Richie shook his head. 'That the grass may grow up over that mean ould culchie's head and swally her!' he prayed.

Whacker laughed. 'Yer man beyond is no culchie,' he said, 'but he ran us just as fast. "I have my own gardener," says he, real grand.'

'Ah, he was ould,' said May. 'Let's see how Mickser and Imelda got on.'

At the third house, they saw an elderly woman standing in the open doorway, as Mickser and Imelda came out carrying garden tools. She smiled and waved to them to wheel their bikes in through the gate, to where Mickser's and Imelda's were already propped against the wall.

'Come on!' Mickser called to them, dumping a fork and a trowel at the bottom of the steps. 'we've to carry the grass cutter through the hall so as not to be destroyin' the floor.'

Wiping their feet carefully on the front door mat,

the others followed him through the hall, down some steps and out the back, where a shed stood with its door ajar. While the boys manhandled the old-fashioned mowing machine, with its heavy wooden rollers, through the house, the girls brought out a pair of hedge clippers, some long border clippers, a yard brush, a watering can and some twine.

'She'll give us a tenner if we make a good job of the front and back,' Mickser whispered to Richie, as they went back for the step-ladder and the wheel-barrow.

'Great! We're in business so,' said Richie gleefully.

'We'll earn it,' said Whacker less enthusiastically. 'Have you seen the size of the back-garden? We'll be all day at it.'

Mickser nodded. 'She wouldn't go any higher,' he said, 'but she'll give us a bit of dinner and there's six of us. Let's get started.'

The mowing machine was old and heavy but it had been well cared for, with the blades sharpened and oiled since winter, and Whacker soon had it purring along in fine style. Mickser trimmed the edge of the lawn around the beds with the long clippers while Richie clipped the hedge that divided the garden from the one next door.

'Wouldn't you know they'd leave the weedin' to us?' pouted Imelda.

May laughed.

'I don't mind the weedin',' she said. 'You take the

twine and tie back all those long blue flowers that are fallin' over the grass.'

'That's larkspur,' said Maura. 'Me Granny used to have that in her window-box. And them giant fellas is hollyhocks.'

'I hope your Granny didn't have them in her window-box,' said Imelda tartly, 'or she wouldn't see much outa the window.'

'They want tyin' back too,' said May quickly, for she had always to keep the peace between Imelda and Maura. 'And when you've that done you can rake up the hedge clippings. Maura will do the weedin' with me.'

Clipping the top of the hedge on his step-ladder, Richie could see over it into the garden next door. The girl they had talked to was still there, just standing, waiting. She must be able to hear the hedge-clippers, Richie thought, but she never once turned towards him.

She stood unnaturally still, facing the laurel bush half-way down the garden. What was there to look at in the laurel bush that would keep her so still, Richie wondered? Then he remembered that she was blind. Her attention was on the gate beyond the bush, listening for the first sound of approaching foot-steps. She must be standing behind the laurel bush so she could not be seen from the house, Richie thought. She must want to talk to the doctor without Mrs. Coffey knowing.

Suddenly Richie saw her tense. Looking beyond

her, he saw there was someone at the gate. He was delicately built for a man, slim with small hands and feet. He pushed the gate open and walked up the garden path with a graceful swinging walk like that of a dancer. He did not see Linda and she made no attempt to speak to him. Yet she must have heard his footsteps on the gravel path.

Raising his arm in a graceful gesture, the man pressed the doorbell and Richie heard it echo faintly inside in the house. Before he could ring a second time, the door was suddenly jerked open and Richie caught a glimpse of Mrs. Coffey's flat featureless face before the man entered the hall and the door closed behind him.

'Are you day dreamin' or what?' asked Whacker.

'Someone's just arrived next door,' Richie told him, jumping down off the step-ladder.

Maura looked up from her weeding. 'Must be the doctor,' she said.

'That man was never a doctor,' said Richie. 'He had a raggedy ould suit on him and he'd no black bag. Doctors always have black bags with them to carry their thermometers and stethoscopes and boxes of pills. He looked more like a dancer.'

'A dancer? What would a dancer be doin' next door?' asked May.

'I dunno,' said Richie. 'It's only that he moved like a dancer. Ring the bell there, Imelda, 'til we tell this ould wan we're ready to start work out the back.'

2   Each shall have a Share

When the old lady opened the door to them, she seemed pleased with the work they had done on the front garden.

'Go on out and get started on the back,' she said, 'and I'll give you a call when I have your lunch ready. See how much you can have done by then.'

There was a lot more grass in the back than in the front garden as Whacker was quick to point out. There was plenty of hedge too, and a great many beds for weeding. There were also rows of lettuces and cabbages, with borders of parsley and bushes of thyme, sage and rosemary. Right at the bottom of the garden, against the far wall, were raspberries, gooseberries and blackcurrants. Mickser looked at them greedily.

'One of you can do the borders if you like,' said Mickser generously to the girls, 'and I'll do the weedin' at this end.'

'Sorra much weedin' you'd do,' May answered scornfully, 'only eat all the fruit on her. We're here to work, not rob.'

'Perks of the job,' retorted Mickser. 'I'll bet it's only what she expects.'

But Whacker sided with May. 'If she finds we've nicked the fruit on her she'll likely take it out of the tenner,' he said. 'We're not boxin' the fox now. Get goin' on them borders.'

Luckily the garden had not been left to run wild like the one beside it and they had it more than half done when the old lady called them in for their bit of lunch. She came down the garden path and glanced swiftly at the fruit bushes.

'We didn't touch the fruit,' Whacker said quickly, 'but it's wantin' pickin' or the birds will have it all on you.'

The old lady smiled. 'When you've the garden finished you can pick what's ready and I'll give you your share. Now come on in and wash your hands before the tea's stewed.'

On the scrubbed wooden table in the old flagged kitchen she had set out a large sliced pan, an old-fashioned crock of yellow butter and red cheddar cheese on a board. The hard work had made them hungry and the pan began to disappear fast.

'We're eatin' all before us,' said May uneasily. 'Is this all the bread you have in the house?'

The old lady laughed. 'Plenty more where that came from,' she said 'They're not short of a few bob.'

'They?' asked Richie, puzzled. 'Is it not your house then?'

'Bless you, no!' said the old lady. 'I'm only the housekeeper here.'

'Will they not mind you gettin' us to do the garden so?' asked Maura anxiously, beginning to wonder had the old lady the ten pounds to give them at all.

'They'll be charmed,' the old lady assured them. 'They're away in Italy on their holidays and they'll expect everything in order for them when they come back. I was expecting the gardener on Tuesday but he never showed up.'

'Maybe he's sick,' suggested Imelda.

'Maybe he is, for he's an elderly man,' the house-keeper agreed, leaving May to wonder how old the gardener could be if he seemed elderly to this wrinkled old woman with her grey hair tidied away under an invisible hair net.

'Anyway, it was a good day that brought you,' continued the housekeeper, 'for there's plenty of growing on that grass yet.'

'You should see it next door,' said Richie. 'It's near up to your knees.'

The old woman nodded. 'Poor old Mr. Mooney would be heart-scalded if he could see it,' she said. 'He looked after that garden himself like a child and always had it beautiful. But since the day he took ill the place has gone to rack and ruin.'

'Mooney?' echoed Maura. 'But I thought the name was Coffey? The girl there called the woman Mrs. Coffey.'

'A cousin of the old man, or so she gives out,' said the housekeeper, 'though it's hard to believe she could be anything to such a soft-spoken old gentle-man, with her rough ways. She arrived shortly before he took ill and she'd hardly her foot in the door before she had everyone run out of it.'

'You mean Linda's mother and father?' asked Maura. 'But sure she couldn't run them, could she?'

'Linda's mother and father were killed in a car accident in England last year,' the old lady said. 'That's why Linda came here to her grandfather. But there was a woman working in the house for years, a good friend of mine that many a time took tea with me in this very kitchen. But whatever way that Mrs Coffey managed things, she had her out of it in jigtime.'

'I feel sorry for Linda,' said Maura, 'with her parents dead, her grandfather sick and only that old Sourpuss for company.'

'And being blind with it,' added Richie. 'No wonder she's nothing to do only hang around waitin' for the doctor.'

'If he *is* a doctor at all,' put in May.

'Ah, you may well say that,' agreed the housekeeper. 'Didn't old Dr. Meath always call to Mooneys, the same as he does here? What call had she to be getting in a stranger?'

Maura was about to tell her how he had had no black bag with him that morning, when the housekeeper pushed back her chair from the table and stood up.

'Well,' she said, 'whatever about Linda, we have more to do than sit around gossiping all day. I've my work to do and you'd best be getting on with the garden.'

While she fought with the roots of a particularly

tough dandelion May thought about the girl next door. From what Richie and Maura had said, she sounded terribly lonely. It must be awful to come to a strange country and have no friends.

'What would I do, all on my own if I couldn't see?' she thought, but of course she would always have Patchie. Dogs were great company, and Patchie always got so worried if ever you were sick or hurt, licking your hand and putting his forepaws up against your chest. If Linda had a dog itself, May thought, she might be less lonely.

They had left Patchie at home that day because they had thought that maybe people might not like to have him too digging in their garden. May thought she might ask Linda before they left if she would like them to bring Patchie with them tomorrow and leave him with her in her garden while they worked further up the road. Once Patchie knew Linda was a friend, he wouldn't make strange.

Suddenly, May heard footsteps and the creak of an outhouse door on the other side of the wall.

'Haven't I already searched in here till I'm blue?' a woman's voice complained, and a man's voice replied sharply.

'You'll be more than blue unless you find it, for if you think I'll wed a pauper you've another think coming.'

Then the shed door creaked to again.

May squatted back on her heels, the dandelion still in her hand, staring at the wall. The voices came from next door, there was no mistaking that, but who could the speakers be? The first voice must have been Mrs.Coffey, but the man could hardly be the sick grandfather.

Maura, weeding amongst the roses, noticed May had stopped work. 'What's wrong?' she called over to her.

May was about to call back when it struck her that if she could hear Mrs. Coffey, Mrs. Coffey might be able to hear her. Instead she went over to Maura's side and whispered to her what she had overheard.

To her surprise, Maura whispered back in triumph, 'So now we know who he is! He's Mrs. Coffey's boyfriend.'

'Who is?' asked May, puzzled.

'The Dancer!' Maura told her. 'Didn't I tell you he was no doctor? They've codded poor Linda that he's the doctor because she's blind and can't see he's no bag with him. And all the time she's worryin' about her grand-da.'

'Then we must tell her the truth,' May decided.

Maura looked unhappy. 'It's nothing got to do with us,' she said. 'We're only workin' here today. Tomorrow we'll be further on up the road. And people won't give us work if we're gonna be pokin' our noses into their business all the time.'

'Mrs. Coffey wouldn't give us work anyway, and I'm not seein' poor Linda made an eejit of, just because she's blind,' said May. 'Let's get finished up here and go and see her.'

'I dunno is it a good idea,' said Maura uneasily. Linda had seemed nice enough, but she was nothing to them and Maura's mother would never let her stay with the others if the gardening was not bringing in enough. She would have to go off on her own cleaning and there would be no fun in that.

'Let's see what the others think,' said May.

'All right,' agreed Maura unenthusiastically, 'but let's get the ten pound first.'

When they had the back garden looking neat and tidy, they went into the kitchen to get baskets for the fruit. The bushes turned out to be heavier than they had realized, but when they dumped the baskets down on the kitchen table, hot and exhausted, there was another pot of tea waiting for them. Better still, they found they had earned themselves an extra two pounds and, while they drank the tea, the house-keeper filled some plastic bags with fruit for them to take home with them.

Suddenly something struck May. 'Are there raspberries and black currants and goosegogs next door?' she asked.

'Ah, no,' the housekeeper said. 'Old Mr. Mooney never bothered with soft fruit. I suppose being on his own he didn't think it was worth the trouble. He has a few apple and pear trees, and a plum tree along the wall, but no soft fruit.'

'Then I'm gonna ask Linda would she like a few raspberries,' said May.

'Ah now, hold on!' protested Mickser. 'That fruit belongs to all of us.'

'Then she can have my share,' said May.

Maura shifted uneasily on her chair. She wanted to say 'and mine too,' but she had been thinking that her share of the fruit might help her mother to overlook the fact that there was only two pounds to show for a whole day's work.

'That's a kind thought,' the housekeeper said. 'If you'll take them round to her, I'll put a few extra into a bag for her.'

'You'd better take them, Maura,' said May, as

they all stopped outside the gate of the next door house. 'She knows you.'

'It was your idea!' objected Maura. 'You'd better come too.'

'I think we should all go,' said Whacker. 'Then we can decide whether to tell her about the doctor.'

'Right,' said Richie. 'Come on then!' and he led the way up the footpath and across the grass towards the corner behind the laurel bush where Linda had been standing, but there was no one there. The front garden was empty!

'She musta gone back into the house,' he said.

'Then we'll ask for her,' said Whacker, marching up the steps to the front door.

Maura and Richie exchanged glances. Whacker had never met Mrs. Coffey. Still, this time they were not looking for anything.

Whacker pushed the bell and they all listened to the familiar echoing jangle, but this time there was no delay.

The door seemed to fly open and Mrs. Coffey darted forward, pushing them away from the door-step like so many hens from around a barn door.

'I told ye to be off about your business. There's no work for ye here,' she shouted angrily.

'We've come to see Linda,' said Whacker stolidly.

'Linda wouldn't be wantin' to see the likes of you,' Mrs. Coffey snapped, trying to close the door, but Whacker's foot was in the way.

'We've something to give her, from the lady next

door,' May added quickly.

'Then ye can leave it with me,' and Mrs. Coffey held out one of her big thick hands for the bag that May was clutching.

Whacker shook his head.

'It's for Linda herself,' he said.

'Then ye can keep it,' said Mrs. Coffey, giving Whacker's ankle a sharp kick that made him cry out in hurt surprise and fall back enough for her to slam the door shut once more.

'You see,' said Richie. 'I told you what she was like.'

'You shoulda let me give it to her,' protested May. 'Now there's no way of gettin' it to Linda.'

'If you'd trust a mean ould wan like that you want yer head seen to,' said Whacker. 'She'd eat the lot herself.'

'Or share them with the boyfriend, maybe,' said Maura. 'But Linda would never get to see them.'

'So what do we do now?' asked Imelda.

'Let's go home,' said Mickser. 'We can share hers out between the rest of us.'

'We'll give them to her tomorrow,' said Whacker. He turned from the door, nursing his ankle, and they all started back down the steps into the garden.

Suddenly they became aware of a gentle steady drumming sound coming from a window at garden level, beside the front door steps.

Through the window, May could see a girl in dark glasses, her cheek up against the pane and her fingers tapping on the glass in a steady rhythm: tap, tap, tap; tap, tap, tap.

'Is that Linda?' she asked.

Maura nodded.

'Sh!' hissed Richie. 'Don't pretend to notice. I think she's signallin' to us. Is anyone watchin'?'

They all looked up at the house, but the upstairs windows seemed blank.

'I think the coast is clear,' Whacker said.

'Then keep in against the side of the steps,' Richie instructed, 'the way we won't be seen from upstairs.'

Following him cautiously into the shadow of the steps, where ivy clung to the wall, they all stood facing Linda through the window. Richie put his hand up to the pane and drummed his fingers softly on the glass, following the same rhythm that Linda had used: tap, tap, tap; tap, tap, tap.

The girl's lips curved in a smile. She slid back the window catch and gently eased the bottom of the window upwards. Then she put a warning finger to her lips and beckoned.

With a quick glance around to make sure no one was looking, Richie climbed in through the window. The others followed, except for Maura. She hesitated for a second, afraid of getting into fresh trouble. Then she heard footsteps on the road outside.

Suppose someone caught her standing by the open window? They might think she was a robber. She plunged hastily in after the others.

34

3   In and Out the Windows

The room they were in had a table in the centre covered with a heavy fringed green baize cloth and four chairs grouped around it. Under the window was a shabby old horsehair sofa, and on either side of the fireplace were equally shabby armchairs. Two things seemed odd about the room. It was unexpectedly dowdy for a room in so fine a house, and it had nothing about it to suggest that anyone had ever lived there. There were no photographs or personal knick-knacks; just a large ashtray with the name of a beer on it, that looked as if it had originally belonged to a pub.

'Is this yer room?' asked Whacker, looking around curiously as Linda closed the window behind them.

Linda turned quickly at the sound of a strange voice. Maura took her hand and placed it on Whacker's chubby face.

'This is Whacker,' she said.

'Hullo, Whacker,' said Linda. 'And who are the other three?'

'How did you know there was six of us?' Maura asked.

Linda smiled. 'I can hear even if I can't see,' she said. 'And the springs on the sofa creaked six times as you dropped down on to it.'

'You don't miss much!' said Whacker in admiration. 'This is me sister Imelda, and this is Richie's sister, May. . .'

'You do it like this' interrupted Richie, pushing each girl in turn in front of Linda, so she could trace their features with her fingers while he repeated their names, and then did the same for Mickser. 'Now you know us all,' he said.

'Yes' said Linda, 'and thanks for dropping in.'

Whacker laughed. 'That's a good one,' he said. 'Droppin' in! We did that all right!'

'We have something for you,' said May. 'Raspberries from the housekeeper next door.'

'Oh, lovely!' said Linda. 'Isn't she kind? We can all have some. Help yourselves.'

Mickser's hand was already reaching for the bag when May slapped it away. 'Don't be a greedy gut! We've got our own. These are for Linda.'

'We'll share them,' said Linda, taking the bag from May's fingers. Deftly she divided the raspberries into seven little piles on the baize-covered table. Again Whacker was impressed by the ease with which she could do things without seeing. 'I want us to be friends,' she added.

'No problem,' said Whacker grandly, as they made short work of the raspberries. 'Is this yer room?'

Linda shook her head.

'It was Lizzie's,' she said. 'Not her bedroom —

she slept up on the top floor — but her sitting-room.'

'Who's Lizzie?' asked Imelda.

'She used to do the cooking and cleaning for my grand-dad until Mrs. Coffey came. I wish she hadn't left. She was always so nice to me and never minded if I sat in here with her when grand-dad was out. But Mrs. Coffey gave her the sack when he got ill. She doesn't want anyone else in the house, except the doctor.'

The others looked at each other and even Maura knew that Linda would have to be told.

'That's why I knew she wouldn't let you in,' went on Linda, 'so when she made me come into the house I slipped down here and waited for you. She thinks I'm upstairs in my room.'

So Linda *had* been hiding behind the laurel bush, thought Richie.

'Why did she make you come in?' he asked.

'She saw from a window that I was waiting for the doctor,' said Linda. 'She never wants me to talk to him.'

'That's because she doesn't want you to find out he's not a doctor at all,' said Richie.

'Oh, but he is!' exclaimed Linda. 'He's been to see my grand-dad every day since he got ill.'

'Maybe he has,' said Maura, 'but he's no doctor. He has no black bag.'

'But then who is he?' Linda asked.

'I think he's Mrs. Coffey's boy friend,' said May, and she told Linda what she had overheard while she was weeding the cabbage patch.

'So that's why she's always moving things around,' said Linda. 'I thought she did it to spite me.'

'How d'ya mean, to spite you?' asked Mickser.

'I knew exactly where everything was in every room,' Linda explained. 'That's how I could always find things when I wanted them, and could walk around without bumping into things. But since Mrs. Coffey came I never know where anything is. She keeps moving everything about in all the rooms. When I asked her about it she said it was because she was turning the rooms out, that Lizzie never cleaned the place properly and that's why she had to go. But that isn't true. Lizzie was always cleaning but she put everything back where it was afterwards.'

'I think Mrs. Coffey moves things around because she's searchin' for something,' May declared.

'But what could she be looking for?' Linda asked.

'Something the Dancer wants her to find,' said Maura.

'The Dancer?' echoed Linda, puzzled. 'Who's the Dancer?'

'Mrs. Coffey's boy friend,' Maura told her. 'The one she's pretendin' is the doctor. We call him that because he looks like a dancer.'

'But if he's not a doctor, why does he go every day to see my grand-dad?' asked Linda.

'Are you sure he does?' Richie asked in reply.

'Oh yes,' said Linda. 'I hear him in his room. And sometimes my grand-dad gives a sort of a moan. I thought the doctor must be giving him an injection or something.'

'Couldn't you ask your grand-da about it?' suggested May.

Linda shook her head.

'Mrs. Coffey won't let me see him,' she said. 'She keeps his door locked so I can't go in to him. She says he's too ill to see anyone except the doctor.'

'Then we'll only have to find out for ourselves,' said Whacker.

'We don't wanta be pokin' our noses into somebody else's business,' said Maura uneasily.

'Looka!' said Richie. 'There's something wrong in this house and I think we all know it. From the time these two people came here everything has gone wrong.' He held up his hand and as he spoke he ticked off each sentence on his fingers. 'Linda's grand-da got sick. Linda isn't let see him. Lizzie was run out of the house. And Linda has no one but us to turn to.' He paused for a moment and said quietly, 'Hands up anyone that wants to help her.'

Five hands shot up followed, after a pause, by Maura's.

'Then that's all of us,' announced Richie.

For a moment May was afraid that Linda was going to cry, but instead she just gulped and said, 'Thanks awfully,' in a very English sort of way.

'Right,' said Imelda, 'but now what do we do?'

'We find out three things,' said Richie. 'First, what's wrong with Linda's grand-da? Second, why didn't they send for a real doctor if he's so ill? And, third, what is it they're lookin' for?'

'I think it must be money,' said May suddenly. 'The Dancer said he wasn't going to marry a pauper. Bet none of you know what a pauper is.'

'It's someone that's poor,' said Maura, 'like on that old notice they used to have outside the Penny Dinner place.'

'Then the Dancer must think if Mrs. Coffey finds what she's lookin' for she won't be poor any more,' declared Richie.

'You mean, there's treasure buried somewhere in the house?' asked Mickser, suddenly more interested.

Linda looked doubtful. 'I never heard grand-dad say anything about buried treasure,' she said.

'He mightn't know about it,' said May. 'Maybe Mrs. Coffey and the Dancer found out about it, and that's why they came here.'

'Why not?' agreed Whacker. 'Nobody knew there was treasure buried under the Fruit and Vegetable Market till Fatser an' Ferrity-Face came lookin' for it.'

'And we found it,' grinned Mickser. 'Maybe we oughta start lookin' here.'

Richie shook his head. 'I think we oughta talk to Linda's grand-da first,' he said.

'But Mrs. Coffey won't let you,' Linda said. 'If

she even catches you in here there'll be an awful row.'

'We won't ask her permission,' grinned Richie. 'We'll just make sure she and the Dancer are somewhere else at the time.'

'What are you at, Redser?' asked Whacker curiously. 'Have you a scheme for gettin' the key offa ould Sourpuss?'

'That might be a bit tricky,' said Richie. 'I thought we might try gettin' in the same way we got in here.'

'You mean, in the window?' Linda exclaimed. 'But grand-dad's room is upstairs!'

'The house is covered in creeper and there's a couple of downpipes. I'm sure we could manage it,' Richie said.

'All of us?' gasped Maura, her face visibly paling.

Richie laughed. 'Just Whacker and me,' he said. 'And maybe Linda.'

'Linda?' echoed Imelda. 'But she can't even see!'

But Linda's face lit up. 'I think I could do it,' she said. 'If I'd someone with me to guide me. I'm the best in my class at gym.'

Richie nodded. 'Then you'd better come,' he said. 'to introduce us, like. Otherwise your grand-da might be scared at two strangers climbin' in through his window.'

'And what do we do while yous are breakin' yer necks?' asked Mickser sourly. Richie always picked Whacker to do everything with him, even though

Whacker was heavier and would put much more strain on a gutter or a downpipe than he would.

'Yous have to be decoys for Sourpuss and the Dancer,' he said. 'To make sure they're well outa the way, while we talk to Linda's grand-da.'

Maura thought uneasily that that was as dangerous as climbing into bedroom windows. She began to wish she had done as her mother told her and gone out cleaning. Why was it, she wondered, that whenever she went anywhere with the Byrnes they always ended up doing something awful?

'Which way does your grand-da's room face?' Richie asked Linda.

'Out over the back garden,' she told him.

'Good for starters!' Richie said. 'We don't wanna be climbing walls in full view of the street. Can you get us out into the back garden so we can take a dekko at the window?'

Linda nodded. 'I think so,' she said, 'if we're quiet. The other two are upstairs and from the noise they're making, they're busy moving everything around again.'

The others had not been aware of any noise, but they fell silent at Linda's words and listened. Then they could just make out a faint bumping and dragging sound, as if drawers and cupboards were being opened and shut, and furniture pushed around, in some far distant room.

'You've great hearing to catch that, and we all talkin',' Whacker said to Linda admiringly.

'If you can't see, you use your ears more.'

'Right,' said Richie. 'We three will slip out the back. The rest of you stand by to cause a distraction.'

'What'll we do?' asked Imelda.

'We could ring the bell again,' suggested Maura hopefully. 'That'd bring her down to the front door and then we could maybe keep her talkin'.'

'Not good enough,' said Whacker. 'She could look outa the window and yell at yous to get lost without even comin' downstairs.'

'And if she did come down the Dancer would still be upstairs,' added Richie. 'You've gotta draw the both of them.'

'We've gotta make them think we're breakin' in, and in two different places,' said May, 'so that it takes the two of them to keep us out. And then we've gotta get them to chase us away from the house.'

'Dead on!' Whacker said. 'One of yous can ring the front doorbell to make sure they hear you and the others can let on to be tryin' to get in by this window and the other one. That oughta draw them.'

'Supposin' they send for the Guards,' said Maura.

'They won't!' Richie said. 'I'm nearly sure of that. They may threaten you with them but whatever they're up to I'm willin' to bet it's something they won't want the Guards askin' questions about.'

'Then maybe we should call the Guards ourselves,' suggested Maura.

The others looked at her as if she had taken leave of her senses.

'D'you think they'd believe anything we'd say against the story Sourpuss and the Dancer would tell?' Richie asked. 'They'd say we were robbin' the place or something. What Guard wouldn't take the word of two grown people in a house like this against a bunch of kids?'

Whacker nodded. 'We'd wanta have proof before we could go to the Guards,' he said. 'Right now, we don't even know what that pair are up to.'

'Maura can be the one that rings the bell,' May said quickly, knowing that Maura was picturing what her mother would do to her if she found out Maura had been caught trying to break into a house. 'And Mickser can do the window on the far side and Imelda and me will do this one.'

'Fair enough,' said Mickser. 'But how will we know when to start? We don't want to be too early or too late.'

'We need some class of a signal,' Richie said.

Suddenly May grinned. 'I know!' she cried triumphantly. 'Whacker can do Patchie!'

Linda looked puzzled.

'Our dog,' May explained to her. 'Whacker can bark just like him. He's always doin' it lately to fool us.'

'Dead on!' said Richie. 'As soon as we're ready to go, Whacker will bark like Patchie. That'll be Maura's signal to ring the front door bell.'

Maura looked worried. 'Supposin' I don't hear him?' she asked.

'You'll hear me all right,' Whacker said. 'I'll do it real loud!'

'Right,' said Richie. 'Let's go. You lot first.'

One by one, Mickser and the three girls climbed up on to the sofa and out of the window.

'We'll leave the window a bit open,' Richie whispered to May and Imelda when they were outside once more, 'so you two can easy push it up again. Make as much noise as you can when you do it. Now hide until you hear the signal.'

Richie watched until all four had disappeared behind the laurel bush. Then he slid the window quietly down until there was just room for the two girls to slip their hands underneath.

'Now!' he said to Linda. 'How do we get out the back?'

Linda led them out of the door and into a flagged passage, exactly like the one in the house next door. The two houses were just the same, Richie thought, except that everything in this one was the other way round.

As he tiptoed softly after her, he thought once again how easily Linda moved around despite not being able to see. She needed only to run her hand along the outside of the cupboard under the stairs to be sure that she was on course. Fortunately there was no furniture here that might have been moved from its usual position to confuse her.

When they reached the back door, Richie could see the door was bolted. He put a restraining hand on

Linda's shoulder and jerked his head at Whacker to come forward. Then the two of them simultaneously eased back the bolt and lifted the latch as silently as possible. Even so the door creaked as they pulled it open and they froze for a moment, listening for signs that they had been heard, but the overhead bumping and clattering continued uninterrupted.

'It's OK,' breathed Whacker. 'They're making too much noise themselves. Come on!'

They were in the back garden now, beside a shed like the one next door. It ran alongside the garden wall and Richie guessed this must have been where Sourpuss and the Dancer were when May overhead them. He said in a whisper to Linda, 'Which is your grand-da's window?'

'It's right above us now,' Linda whispered back.

'That first one there?' asked Whacker. 'That's easy!'

Linda shook her head. 'Not that one,' she said. 'That's the dining-room. It's the one above that again.'

Richie looked up at the face of the building before him. Whereas the front of the building was all red brick, the back walls were just smooth plaster that gave no hope of a foothold. It would be easy enough to reach the dining-room window from the top of the shed, but then they would still only be at hall door level.

'Maybe we could use the downpipe on the return,' he thought to himself.

The return, where the bathroom and toilet were, had been built on to the house at a later stage. Richie guessed the doors from them gave on to the stair landings. Drainpipes ran up the side of the return building. Where these joined the downpipe, they formed a kind of funnel, which might support a climber.

'Well, Redser, what's the plan?' asked Whacker.

'We get on to the shed roof and then cross to the pipe by the dining-room window sill,' Richie told him.

'Shall I give the signal?' Whacker asked.

Richie hesitated. 'We're gonna need as much time as possible,' he said. 'Let's get as far as the shed roof first.'

'Supposin' they look outa the window?' Whacker asked.

'They're on the other side of the house,' Linda said. 'In the sitting-room, I think. They sounded louder on that side anyway.'

'Good enough, so,' said Richie. 'Let's get the shed door open.'

Using the top of the door to lever himself up, Richie quickly swung himself on to the shed roof.

'Now, Linda,' he whispered. 'Give her a boost, Whacker!'

Whacker placed Linda's hands on top of the door and put her left foot on his knee. 'Right,' he whispered. As she hauled herself up, Richie grabbed her and guided her on to the shed roof beside him. Then,

as Whacker prepared to follow them, Linda suddenly clutched Richie's arm.

'They've come into the dining-room!' she whispered. 'I know the sound the dining-room door makes!'

'Quick, Whacker! The signal!' Richie whispered frantically.

Whacker threw back his head and the sound of a small dog barking hysterically echoed off the walls of the house.

Only then did the danger strike Richie.

'Look out!' he hissed, pushing Linda back against the wall of the house. Even as he did so, the face of Mrs. Coffey appeared at the window. Richie held his breath. If she turned her head sharply enough, she would surely see them.

She looked out straight in front of her, searching for a small dog with a loud bark that had somehow got into their garden. Richie stood tense, waiting for the angry shout when she saw Whacker. Then the door bell jangled loudly.

4 Steady on the Stair

At the sound of the doorbell, Mrs. Coffey's face disappeared from the window and Richie gave a sigh of relief. He peered anxiously down over the side of the shed in time to see Whacker emerging cautiously.

Good old Whacker, thought Richie. He had guessed his dog act would attract attention and slipped inside and closed the door.

Richie waved to him that the coast was clear and Whacker heaved himself up on to the roof beside them. But the roof was never built to stand the weight of three people. Suddenly there was an ominous cracking sound.

'Quick! Over here!' hissed Richie, stepping quickly back on to the high garden wall that formed the back wall of the shed. There was a loud crack as one section of galvanized iron bent in under Whacker's weight and, for a second, he teetered off balance. Then Richie gave him a yank forward that sent him sprawling on his face, his hands clutching the edge of the wall.

For a moment Richie was afraid the whole section of roof would cave in. Then he realized that Whacker's weight lying down was more evenly distributed, some of it being taken by the next section of roof and some by the wall.

'Crawl!' he hissed urgently, 'but slowly!'

Inch by inch Whacker eased his weight off the sagging roof until he was beside Richie and Linda on the wall. Cautiously, Richie helped him to his feet.

'Whacker put his foot through the shed roof!' he whispered to Linda.

'So I heard,' she giggled. 'Will the drainpipe be strong enough to hold him?'

'We'll only have to hope for the best,' he said. 'But first we'd better make sure they're not still in the dining-room.'

'Listen,' said Linda, 'and you'll hear!'

Then Richie realized that worrying over Whacker and the shed roof had made him deaf to the hubbub going on at the front of the house. People were yelling, doors were banging and feet were pounding on the gravel. It was not surprising no one heard the roof give way.

'I hope our side's winning!' grinned Whacker.

'No time to think about it now,' said Richie. 'Come on. Same order as before,' and he climbed out on to the dining-room window-ledge that was beside and slightly above the shed roof. Holding on to the window frame for support with his right hand, he reached his left back for Linda. She put her right foot out into space, searching with it for the ledge, her weight still on her left foot.

'Up a bit', urged Whacker.

While Richie waited for Linda to join him on the window-ledge, he glanced into the dining-room.

What he saw made him catch his breath with excitement.

As Linda found the ledge, swung herself on to it and shuffled along it towards him, Richie gripped her hand. 'Would the key to your grand-da's room be on a bunch with a whole clatter of keys?' he asked.

Linda nodded. 'Mrs. Coffey has them all on a huge ring,' she said, 'just like a gaoler.'

'They're sittin' on the dining-room table now,' Richie told her.

'What's wrong?' asked Whacker, as he joined them on the ledge.

'Change of plan,' announced Richie. 'We're goin' in through this window.' He pointed to the bunch of keys on the table. 'Mrs. Coffey musta forgot them when she heard Mickser and the girls. Come on. Let's get this window open.'

The two boys slid up the bottom half of the window and the three of them dropped down into the room. Grabbing the bunch of keys Richie ran to the door, eased it open cautiously and peered out.

He could see the Dancer's back in the hallway by the open front door.

'If you don't clear off immediately,' he was saying angrily, 'I'll call the Guards. I'm a doctor and I've a patient seriously ill upstairs. A disturbance like this could make the difference between life and death.'

'Lead the way,' Richie whispered. Linda ran on tiptoe up the stairs to the room immediately above the dining-room.

Richie tried one of the keys. It slid in easily enough, but it did not turn the lock.

'Hurry up!' whispered Whacker urgently. Even as he spoke, there came a fresh outburst of shouting from downstairs, and the sound of feet running on gravel.

'Let's hope Sourpuss chases after them,' said Richie. Then suddenly he found the right key and the lock turned.

Like a hare, Linda was into the room and across to the old-fashioned bed with its brass knobs at the four corners. The two boys followed, closing the door gently behind them. An old man lay slumped in the bed, his body like that of a child under the enormous quilt. His face was almost as white as the pillow beneath his head and he was looking up at Linda with eyes that seemed to burn feverishly.

'Grand-dad!' she cried, as she ran her fingers lightly over his face. 'Oh, grand-dad! What have they done to you?'

The old man clutched at Linda and clung to her with surprising strength for one who looked so weak and pale.

'Linda,' he mumbled. 'I thought you'd left me!'

Richie and Whacker felt embarrassed, standing awkwardly looking on. Linda must have sensed the way they felt, for she put out a hand and drew Richie to the bedside. 'This is Richie, grand-dad. And the other one's his friend, Whacker.'

But the old man seemed unable to take this in. He

never shifted his gaze from Linda's face and Richie began to think that he need not have worried about alarming the old man by their strange entrance. He was almost sure the old man did not even know they were there.

'I thought you'd gone,' he repeated in a low tone. 'Gone and left me with those two.'

'They said you were too ill to see me,' said Linda.

'You gone! Lizzie gone!' said the old man. He seemed unable to think of anything else. Richie was beginning to be afraid that they would learn nothing from him. There was no doubt that he was ill. Whatever might be wrong with his body, his mind seemed to be very confused.

'They sent Lizzie away,' Linda said. 'They said you told them to.'

'Told them?' echoed the old man, suddenly agitated. 'I told them nothing and they won't make me. No matter what they do to me.'

Richie and Whacker looked at each other. All of a sudden Linda's grand-da was sounding like something out of a spy series on the telly. Was it just his mind wandering or did he really know something? But what on earth could an old man like that know that would be of interest to Sourpuss and the Dancer? He certainly did not look like a character out of a spy series.

'What do they want you to tell?' asked Richie, but the old man ignored him. His mind was concentrated entirely on Linda.

'I'll tell those robbers nothing,' the old man said again. He was still very agitated and his voice shook. 'Wasn't it on account of them I hid it? You won't tell them, will you, Linda? Promise me you won't tell?'

'Tell them what?' asked Whacker with interest, but he too might never have existed.

'Of course, I promise,' said Linda soothingly, and the old man seemed somewhat reassured.

'Then you'll be all right,' the old man said. 'I've left it all to you. Just remember the crossword, then two down and four across.'

'All right, grand-dad,' Linda said gently. 'Now we'll get you a proper doctor.'

The effect of her words on the old man was startling. His eyes bulged and his hands groped frantically.

'No doctor,' he babbled. 'You promised!'

'A *different* doctor, grand-dad,' said Linda, but the old man was not calmed.

'Say it!' he demanded, his hands clutching at Linda in his distress 'Say it!'

Remembering how she had calmed him before, Linda repeated, 'I promise not to tell them,' but this time her words did not have the same effect.

'What?' gasped the old man. He was making a terrible effort and beads of perspriation covered his face. 'Promise not to tell them what?'

Linda did not know what to say for the best. She knew he was getting more and more excited, for she could hear it in his voice and feel the sweat on his brow. But what could she do to calm him?

'The crossword!' the old man insisted frantically. 'Two down and four across. Say it!'

Linda had no idea what he was talking about, but if repeating this gibberish would help she would do it gladly. 'The crossword,' she echoed. 'Two down and four across.'

Still the old man did not relax. He made one more gigantic effort, pulling his wasted body up off the pillows to hold Linda to him.

'And you won't tell?' he insisted, his eyes searching her face.

'I won't tell,' Linda repeated. 'I promise.'

The old man gave a great sigh of relief that seemed to come from deep down inside him. Then he fell back on to the pillow. He looked very peaceful now, Richie thought. He even seemed to be smiling.

Linda ran her fingers over his face and smiled too. She was glad now that they had come because, for some strange reason, she had made her grand-dad happy. Until now she had been afraid Mrs. Coffey had been right in telling her she would only make him worse if she saw him. But Linda could not see the strange fixed stare in her grandfather's eyes.

Whacker and Richie exchanged glances. Then Richie put his hand on Linda's shoulder. 'Better leave now, Linda,' he said.

'But we only just got here,' Linda said. 'I want to stay with him now. He wants me here.'

Whacker gently closed the old man's eyes.

'There's nothing he wants now,' he said.

'What do you mean? Is he asleep?' asked Linda, running her fingers across the old man's face again, but this time she felt the lifelessness beneath her hands. 'Is he dead?' she cried.

Richie put an arm awkwardly across her shoulders. 'He's at peace now,' he said. But Linda could not keep back the tears.

'Don't cry,' said Richie, embarrassed. 'He's better off.'

'I know,' sobbed Linda. 'I'm crying for myself. I've no one in the whole world now.'

'Of course, you have,' said Whacker stolidly. 'You have all of us.'

Then they heard the sound of feet on the stairs and the Dancer's voice saying, 'There are your keys! You left them in the old man's door.'

'That's funny!' Mrs. Coffey was saying. 'I could have sworn I brought them downstairs with me!'

'Quick!' said Richie. 'Behind the door!'

Pulling Linda off the bed, the two boys pushed her back against the wall, standing either side of her, so that they would be hidden from anyone coming into the room.

The door opened, and they pressed themselves flat against the wall, hardly daring to breathe. They heard Mrs. Coffey's voice on the far side of the door.

'I do believe the old divil's managed to go asleep!'

Then they heard a man's voice. It was soft, yet there was something terrifying about it too.

56

'Don't worry, I'll soon wake him up. And this time I'll get it out of him all right.'

'Wait now till I tie this around his mouth to stifle his screaming!' Then Mrs. Coffey screamed herself, 'He's dead!'

'Are you sure?' The man's voice was sharper now. He joined Mrs. Coffey at the bedside.

Richie tapped Linda on the shoulder.

'Now!' he breathed. He leaped out from behind the door and raced after Whacker on to the landing and down the stairs.

Linda hesitated. Even if her grandfather were dead, she found it hard to leave him in the hands of the Dancer. Then she felt Mrs. Coffey's powerful hands gripping her below the shoulders.

'And where do you think you're away to, my lady?' she asked.

'You can't leave her running wild with a bunch of young hooligans, Mrs. Coffey,' added the soft voice of the Dancer. 'A poor blind girl lost on the city streets at this hour of the evening! If she hasn't the sense to stay at home we must protect her for her own good. I suggest you lock her in her room at once.'

It was useless to struggle. Mrs. Coffey's hands held her like a vice. Linda was dragged to her room and flung across the bed.

'You can stay here till you learn to mind your business and do as you're told,' said Mrs. Coffey.

Linda heard the door slam behind her. The key turned in the lock. She was a prisoner.

5   Round and Round the Garden

As they reached the front door, Richie realized that Linda was not with them.

'Linda ...' Richie gasped. 'We can't leave her here.'

'We won't help her by getting caught ourselves,' panted Whacker wrenching open the door.

'And you won't help her by informing either.'

The unexpected words made the boys swing round. The Dancer was standing on the landing looking down at them.

'One word of this to anyone and I won't answer for her safety,' he added. 'I'm sure you wouldn't want to cause her to have an accident, would you?'

There was something so awful about the way he spoke that it seemed to take the power from their limbs. After seeing the old man, they never doubted that he meant what he said.

'You do understand, I hope?' continued the Dancer, as they stood frozen in the open doorway.

They nodded, dumbly. Then they fled down the garden path. May was waiting for them at the gate.

'Round to the right,' she cried. They pounded after her, across the railway bridge and on towards the shops, where the others were grouped around the six bikes.

'They can't do anything to us here,' May explained. 'There's too many people about.'

'I doubt they'll try anything for the moment,' Whacker said, his voice finally coming back to him. 'They've enough on their plate.'

'You mean, a body on their hands,' squawked Richie. He still felt as if there was a large lump in his throat.

'A b-b-b-body?' echoed Maura, going white in the face.

'Linda's grand-da's dead,' Richie said flatly.

'Oh, poor Linda!' cried Maura. 'Is that why she didn't come with you?'

Richie shook his head. 'It's worse than that,' he said with difficulty. 'I think they're holdin' her as a sort of hostage.'

'A hostage?' Imelda looked at him blankly. 'But why?'

'So we can't go to the Guards,' Whacker told her. 'The Dancer said if we say a word to anyone something could happen her.'

'They wouldn't dare!' gasped May.

'Wouldn't they though?' said Richie. 'Linda thinks they killed her grand-da.'

'You m-m-m-mean, they m-m-m-m-murdered him?' asked Maura, her voice shaking.

'Well, kind of, though maybe not meanin' to,' Whacker said, and told them everything that had happened.

'Oh, what are we gonna do?' wailed Maura, when

he had finished the grim tale. 'We can't leave Linda with that awful man!'

'I dunno,' said Whacker seriously. 'But we can't go back now. They'd be ready for us. And they won't harm Linda so long as they think they've scared us off.'

Richie nodded. 'Whacker's right,' he said. 'It's near tea-time and Maura's Ma will start sendin' out search-parties if we're late back. After tea we'll meet in the Square and work out a proper plan. Then we'll take them by surprise.'

It seemed the only thing to do. No one was happy about leaving Linda, but what Whacker and Richie had said made sense. Sourpuss and the Dancer would be ready and waiting for them now and, if anything went wrong, who could say what they might do to Linda?

In poor spirits, they set off through Phibsboro'. All the way back they hardly spoke.

Maura's mother was in the kitchen getting the tea when she arrived back.

'Well?' was the question as she came in. 'What did you get?'

'Two pound,' said Maura, putting the money down on the kitchen table. 'and some raspberries and goosegogs.' It seemed a long time ago that they had picked the fruit, so long she hardly cared what her mother thought.

'Payin' you in kind, were they?' commented her mother sharply, but from the look on her face she had been prepared for worse. 'Is there enough in the fruit for jam?'

Maura put the two bags down on the table beside the money and the sight of them seemed to put her mother into good humour.

'You coulda done worse,' she said. 'I'll get a coupla pots of jam outa that lot that'd be the best part of 50p each in the supermarket. Sit down to yer tea.'

The minute she had the washing-up done to her mother's satisfaction, Maura joined the others in the Square. 'Have you made a plan yet?' she asked eagerly.

'We gotta go back and rescue Linda,' said Richie.

'Tonight?' asked Maura doubtfully.

'Tonight,' said Richie. 'And we gotta find whatever it is them two are searchin' for. That's the only way of gettin' rid of them. Otherwise they'll stick around for ever, persecutin' Linda.'

'Wouldn't you think they might scarper now? suggested Imelda hopefully. 'I mean, if they killed Linda's grand-da, wouldn't they wanta get away before they got caught?'

Richie shook his head. 'Everyone knew the ould man was ill in bed, so no one's gonna ask why he's not around,' he said. 'So long as Sourpuss acts normal they're safe. If she scarpers then everyone would start askin' where was the ould lad and who was mindin' him. They'd find out what had happened and there'd be a hue and cry out for both of them.'

Whacker looked at Richie shrewdly. 'What d'ya

think it is they're searchin' for, Redser?' he asked.

'I dunno,' Richie replied, 'but whatever it is, it's something the ould man wanted Linda to have. Remember he said he'd left it for her and he'd hidden it the way them two couldn't get it. "Those robbers", he called them.'

'But if them two can't find it, how d'you think we can?' asked Imelda.

'Specially when we don't even know what it is we're lookin' for,' added Mickser.

Richie looked thoughtful. 'I think Linda's grand-da gave us a clue,' he said. 'If we can only make sense of it. D'you remember what he said, Whacker? About the crossword?'

'He said, "Remember the crossword, two down and four across",' said Whacker. 'But that's only gobbledegook. The poor man was ravin'.'

'I dunno,' said Richie. 'Maybe Linda could make something out of it. I was gonna ask her and then them two came in an' caught us.'

'Would it be a crossword like the ones on the Sunday paper?' asked Maura.

Whacker shrugged. 'That's what we gotta ask Linda, soon as we've rescued her,' he said.

'And how are we gonna do that?' asked Maura, feeling they were no further on than when they had left the North Circular Road.

'We take them by surprise,' said Richie, 'and to do that we gotta play it by ear. Maybe we can use the same trick ... someone lures them outa the house while the others get in and fetch Linda.'

'Come on so,' said Whacker, 'let's get back there,' and they all set off for the North Circular Road once more.

On the way, Maura could think of nothing but Linda. She kept seeing her pale face in front of her. It was terrible to think of her in the hands of such ruthless people. Somehow, the fact that she was not able to see the people that threatened her made it all the more frightening.

They must rescue her and get rid of Sourpuss and the Dancer, so Linda would be safe. But even then she would be all alone in that big old house now her grandfather was dead. She would need someone to keep her company until she went back to school.

I could take care of her myself, thought Maura, if only I hadn't to earn money all the time. She had often prayed that her father would get a job, but that was more because she knew it would make her mother happy and stop the rowing between her parents than for her own sake. Of course, it would be lovely to be able to buy clothes now and then and not to be always worrying about money. Yet things had been that way for so long now that she had almost forgotten how it had been when her father worked as a porter in the Fruit and Vegetable Market.

With a start she realized that they had reached Phibsboro'. There was no point in thinking about the future now. It would need all their plotting to find some way to get Linda out of the hands of Sour-puss and the Dancer.

'The first thing to do is to get rid of the bikes,' said Whacker. 'We wanta have them somewhere near where they'll be safe, so as we can make a quick get-away.'

'How about hidin' them on the railway bank?' suggested Richie. 'It's closer than the shops and no one'll see them there.'

Everyone agreed that this was a good idea and the bikes were soon concealed behind bushes on the grassy slope that ran up from the railway track. Then they approached the house cautiously on foot.

The house was in total darkness, except for a light shining faintly through the curtains of one of the rooms on the hall floor. It was the room immediately over the one which Linda had said had been the housekeeper's room.

'That's the living-room,' whispered Richie. 'They must all be in there.'

No sooner had he spoken than the light in the living-room went out and was replaced by a glow from the fanlight over the hall door. Then a light went on in the room over the sitting-room. Whacker gripped Richie's shoulder.

'That's gotta be Linda's room,' he said. 'The ould man's room is at the back over the dining-room.'

Suddenly something struck Maura. 'Why would Linda want the light on if she can't see anyway?'

Richie nodded excitedly. 'She wouldn't,' he said,

'and you know what that means? Sourpuss must be in there too!'

'What about the Dancer?' asked May.

'He doesn't live here,' said Whacker. 'He only calls every day like a doctor. That's why the light went off in the living-room when Sourpuss went upstairs. She wouldn't have left him sittin' in the dark, so he musta gone home by now.'

'So this is where we go in,' said Richie urgently. 'All we gotta do is trick Sourpuss into opening the door. Have you got Patchie's twine, May?'

May nodded and pulled out of her pocket the bit of twine she always kept for tying Patchie up.

'Right!' said Richie. 'Everyone except Whacker go and hide at the side of the steps.'

'What about me?' asked Whacker.

'You go behind the laurel bush and do your Patchie imitation again,' said Richie. 'Then when she comes lookin' for you, we all spring on her from behind and tie her up!'

'Are you sure she'll come?' asked Whacker. 'I mean, we already pulled that stunt today.'

'That's just why she'll come,' said Richie. 'She'll remember that last time it happened she did nothing about the dog. This time she'll make sure to find out what's happenin'. The minute she comes down the steps, Mickser and I grab her and tie her up.'

'Won't she yell?' asked May.

'That's where you come in,' said Richie. 'You'll have to stuff something into her mouth.'

'I'll use my socks,' said May, slipping her feet out of her shoes and pulling them off. 'Will you help me, Imelda, and then Maura can keep cavey at the gate?'

Imelda nodded.

'Right! Then let's get goin',' said Richie. 'The second we're outa sight, Whacker starts barkin'.'

Maura hesitated. She was grateful to May for letting her off the attack on Sourpuss. In spite of all the awful things that Mrs. Coffey and the Dancer were supposed to have done, she could not help imagining what her mother or the Guards would think of Richie's plan. And suppose they had made a mistake and Sourpuss had not really done those things at all?

Before she could resolve her fears, Whacker began to yap, the way Patchie did when he smelt a rat; excited, shrill, hysterical barking that seemed to go on and on. She looked up and down the road but there was no one about. Then she heard the sound of the front door opening and without knowing what she was doing, she plunged down behind the hedge.

She knew she was supposed to be keeping a look-out, but terror at the thought of what they were about to do made her close her eyes. When she plucked up enough courage to open them again, the garden was empty and silent, except for the sound of scuffling behind the laurel bush. That must be where they were hiding their gagged and bound prisoner, she thought, but she did not want to know anything about that.

66

Suddenly she realized that the front door was open and that the light was still burning in the upstairs room. While the others were busy with Mrs. Coffey, she would rescue Linda. She raced swiftly up the steps and in through the front door.

The staircase was directly in front of her and she made for it without a thought in her head but to reach the room that Whacker had said was Linda's. Then she stopped dead.

Through the bannisters at the head of the stairs she saw a flicker of white. Something was moving towards the staircase — towards her. She stood, frozen in terror, afraid to move up or down, lest she be seen.

Then she gave a gasp and ran upstairs as fast as her legs would carry her.

6 *Like a Dancing Bear*

Linda had lain on her bed for what seemed like hours. At first, she had strained her ears for every movement that would tell her where Mrs. Coffey and the Dancer were.

She had heard them going in and out of her grandfather's room across the landing, and had heard their voices raised in excited talk. Then she had heard their feet descending the stairs. For a long while after that all was silent.

Despair flooded over her. Her grandfather was dead. Her new friends were gone. She herself was a prisoner. She could not bear to think about her troubles so she thought instead about what her grandfather had tried to tell her. What had he meant about the crossword? He had been fond of doing crossword puzzles. When it was raining too hard to work in the garden, he would sit in the living-room doing crosswords. He had a whole book full of them. But what had he meant about remembering two down and four across? It was a mystery, but her grandfather had wanted her to solve it. For his sake she must try. She thought and thought about it until she fell asleep.

She was awakened by the sound of her door being unlocked. At once she was tense, wondering who was there and what new danger threatened. Then she heard the squeak of Mrs. Coffey's shoes and the sound of a tray being set down on the table beside her bed.

'I've brought your tea,' Mrs. Coffey was saying, 'though you don't deserve it.'

'I'm not hungry,' Linda said sullenly. The thought of eating anything prepared by this woman after the way she had spoken of her grandfather turned Linda's stomach.

'Please yourself,' said Mrs. Coffey. 'You'll be sorry after, for you'll get nothing more from me tonight.'

'I don't care,' said Linda. She felt less afraid of Mrs. Coffey when the Dancer was not there and she felt sure he must have gone home long ago.

Suddenly a frenzied yapping could be heard from the direction of the front garden. Linda's heart leaped as she recognized the sound. Whacker must have come back and be trying to signal to her.

Mrs. Coffey heard it too, and she must have noticed Linda's reaction for she said,

'If them young hooligans think they can fool me a second time they're making a bad mistake. That's the same dog that got in the back this evening while the others were out the front. But this time I'll teach him a lesson he'll not forget in a hurry.'

Linda heard Mrs. Coffey cross to the door. The door slammed and Linda waited for the sound of the key turning in the lock, but it never came. Instead,

Mrs. Coffey's footsteps continued along the landing and down the stairs. In her anger Mrs. Coffey had forgotten to lock the door. Linda realized that she was no longer a prisoner!

She slipped out of the bed and tiptoed cautiously to the door. She heard the front door opening and waited for Mrs. Coffey's angry shout or the sound of the others attacking the house, but the yells and sounds of running feet never started. An eerie hush hung over the house.

Linda felt a prickling at the back of her neck, but she knew she must get out of the room while she could. Cautiously she opened the door and began to creep along the landing.

Suddenly she heard the sound of feet on the stairs. She shrank back against the wall. The footsteps stopped. Again she felt the strange, prickling sensation as she stood, not daring to breathe. Then, before she could run, there was a rush of steps and someone grabbed her.

She opened her mouth to cry out, then felt Maura's arms around her and heard Maura's voice crying, 'Linda! Linda! You're safe!' The relief was so great that her legs suddenly seemed to go from under her and she collapsed in Maura's arms on the top step of the stairs.

As they slowly picked themselves up, half-laughing, half-crying, they heard the others come into the house.

'Be careful,' Linda warned. 'Mrs. Coffey . . .'

'It's all right,' Maura said. 'The others have seen to her.'

As Maura and Linda came down the stairs together, the others gave a ragged cheer, but Maura felt it was no time for heroics.

'Let's hurry and get out of this place,' she said. 'We have Linda now.'

Richie shook his head. 'Not' til we've found whatever them two are searchin' for,' he said. 'We've plenty of time. Now it's Sourpuss's turn to wait on us behind the laurel bush, the way Linda used to have to wait for the Dancer.'

'So where do we start to look?' asked Imelda. It seemed an impossible task in that big house.

'I'm hopin' Linda can tell us that,' Richie said.

Linda shook her head. 'I don't even know what it is they're after,' she said, 'much less where it would be.'

'But you know about the crossword, don't you?' Richie persisted. 'Your grand-da thought you did anyway.'

'Only that he has a whole big book full of them,' Linda told him.

'And then there's the bit about two down and four across,' put in Mickser. 'What's that all about?'

'They're just two of the words you'd have to get to fill in the crossword,' Linda explained. 'The word that runs down from number two and the one that runs across from number four.'

'Maybe if we could get a hold of that book with all

the crosswords in it, it'd help,' said Whacker. 'D'ya know where we could find it, Linda?'

'It's on the top bookshelf in the living-room,' said Linda. 'Unless those two moved it.'

'Then we'll start with that,' said Richie. 'It's not much to go on, but it's better than nothing. Come on!'

'This way then,' said Linda, moving as decisively as if she could see her way towards the door on her left.

It led into a large room with bookshelves on either side of the fireplace, flanked by armchairs facing an enormous sofa.

'The crossword book should be here,' said Linda, putting out her left hand to make sure the armchair was where she expected it to be, and passing behind it to the shelving on the right of the fireplace. Then she reached up and took a book from the end of the row on the top shelf. The others inspected it eagerly.

'Collected Crosswords, Volume Two', May read aloud from the cover.

Linda looked relieved. 'Grand-dad always kept it there,' she said, 'only I was afraid Mrs. Coffey might have moved it.'

Richie turned the pages. He was not sure what he had expected to find, but there was nothing; no pages marked or with corners turned down. Nearly all of the crosswords had had letters inserted in the little boxes, but there was nothing that could be called a clue for them.

'There's nothing here,' he said.

'Maybe if you looked up the clues to two down and four across they'd tell you where to find whatever it is,' suggested May.

'But there's hundreds of puzzles,' said Richie. 'And there must be a two down and four across in loads of them.'

'Let's see,' said Mickser.

Richie gave him the book and he started to examine it in detail, watched by the others, except Linda. She seemed to have lost interest in the book and had returned to the bookshelves. May noticed her put her hand into the space where the book had been.

'Is there something stuffed into the back of the shelf?' she asked, wondering why that idea had not occurred to them before. Behind the crossword book would be a good hiding-place, but Linda shook her head.

The others, who had crowded around at May's question, fell back again, but Linda seemed reluctant to give up. She moved her hand down on to the book below the empty space, and then on to the one below that again. Then, as May watched her, she moved her hand sideways on to the fourth book along. It was a heavy, leather-bound book, much bigger than the one with the crosswords, and Linda struggled to lift it down from the shelf.

As May ran to help her, it dropped to the floor with a crash and from it fell a large envelope. May snatched the envelope up and drew from it a type-written manuscript. Peering over her shoulder as she unfolded it, the others read the words at the top of the page:

'I, William Madden Mooney, of The Laurels, North Circular Road, Dublin, hereby revoke all former testamentary dispositions made by me and declare this to be my last Will.'

Richie whistled softly. 'This is it!' he said. 'That's what they were lookin' for. It's Linda's grand-da's Will!'

Linda smiled. 'It was in the book two down and four across from the crossword book,' she said. 'That's just the sort of thing grand-dad would do!'

'But why would Sourpuss and the Dancer make such a song and dance over that?' asked Imelda.

Whacker grinned. 'I bet it leaves everything to Linda,' he said. 'That's what he said just before he talked about the crossword, only we didn't know what he meant.'

Richie, who had continued to puzzle over the funny sentences, full of words like 'hereinafter' and 'heretofore', nodded.

'Listen to this,' he said, and read, ' " I give all the real and personal estate not hereby or by a Codicil hereto otherwise specifically disposed of to my grand-daughter Linda Jones in belated recompense for all the years I neglected her." '

May saw that Linda was crying. 'Poor grand-dad,' she said softly. 'Poor grand-dad.'

'But why would Sourpuss and the Dancer want to find a Will that left everything to Linda?' asked May. 'Or did they think it would leave something to them?'

Whacker shook his head. 'I betcha they wanted to find it so as to burn it,' he said. 'They musta known what was in it and that it'd be found sooner or later unless they got their hands on it.'

'But would that mean they'd get the money instead of Linda?' asked Mickser. 'I mean Linda's a grand-daughter and Sourpuss is only an ould cousin.'

'I was wonderin' about that myself,' Whacker agreed.

But Linda put her hand on Whacker's arm. She had stopped crying now and her voice was full of excitement.

'Supposing there was another Will?' she suggested.

They all looked at her, confused. Then Whacker got the message.

'You mean, leavin' everything to Sourpuss?' he asked.

Linda nodded. 'You see, he quarrelled with my mother,' she explained. 'And all the time we lived in London he never even wrote to us.'

'You mean, you never met him 'til after your Ma and Da died?' May asked.

Linda nodded again. 'He told Mummy if she married my father he never wanted to see her again,' she said. 'Then, when she and Daddy were killed, he felt awful and he said I was to come over here for my school holidays.'

'And he got real fond of you and changed his Will,' said Richie triumphantly.

'And Sourpuss got to hear about it and came here to try to persuade him to change it back and he wouldn't,' cried Whacker. 'I bet that's it.'

'Because the Dancer wouldn't marry her if she was a pauper,' added May, remembering what she had overheard while she was weeding the cabbage patch.

'So when your grand-da got sick they decided to destroy the new Will so that the old one would still count,' continued Richie.

'Only they couldn't find it!' put in Mickser excitedly.

'But we have,' finished Whacker, 'so we've put a stop to their little game.'

'On the contrary!' said a strange voice from behind them.

They all swung round and there stood the Dancer.

7 One Steps, Two Steps

Everyone had been so excited over the finding of the Will that they had never once glanced back towards the open door or noticed the Dancer slip silently in on his rubber-soled shoes. Where he had come from they could not imagine, for there had been no sign of him about the house.

'On the contrary,' he repeated softly, 'you have been of the greatest assistance to us. We have been searching for that piece of paper for some time and without you we might never have found it. Thank you very much!' He held out his hand for it as casually as if he was asking them to pass the milk at the tea table. But something in the soft voice and the casual gesture held a strange menace.

'You're not gettin' it,' cried Richie defiantly, putting his right hand that held the Will behind his back.

'I'm afraid that's where you're quite wrong, young man,' replied the Dancer silkily. 'You're going to hand that document to me. Then you are going to leave this house and remain away from both it and Linda in the future.'

'What makes you think that?' asked Whacker. 'There's seven of us against one. You can't make us do anything.'

The Dancer laughed and the laugh was like that of a vampire in a horror-film. 'Have you forgotten about Mrs. Coffey?'

'We've taken care of her,' said Whacker, 'So you see there's only you against all of us!'

'And you needn't talk about calling the Guards either,' said May. 'We know you don't want them in here askin' questions.'

The Dancer smiled, but the smile never softened the cold, almost hypnotic gaze of his pale blue eyes.

He said, 'You will do exactly what I tell you, for Linda's sake.'

The little bunch closed in protectively around Linda.

'You can't threaten us with harmin' Linda again,' said Richie. 'We won't let you touch her.'

'Such a thought never entered my mind,' replied the Dancer, again smiling that bleak little smile. 'You'll go because Linda herself will beg you to. And beg you to remain silent about everything you have seen and heard in this house.'

'I will not!' cried Linda. 'After all that's happened to my grand-dad I'll do nothing for you.'

'Ah!' said the Dancer, 'but it's what might happen to him in the future that you should think about.'

'You won't trick me like that,' cried Linda. 'D'you think I don't know that he's dead. There's nothing more you can do to him now.'

'My dear child,' said the Dancer patronisingly, 'how dramatic you are! Your grandfather is certainly not dead!'

'But we saw him!' cried Whacker. 'We were there when he died!'

'Your outrageous behaviour in forcing your way into his room certainly did him no good,' the Dancer retorted. 'In fact, it caused him to lapse into a coma which could have very serious results.'

'Is he really still alive?' asked Linda. She seemed torn between her longing to believe that it was true and her distrust of the Dancer.

'He is,' the Dancer said severely, 'though it's no thanks to you and your friends.'

There was a sinking feeling in the pit of Maura's stomach. It was beginning to look as if the Dancer really was a doctor after all! Had they after all caused nothing but harm by interfering? And at this very minute, Sourpuss must by lying behind the laurel bush with her hands tied and May's socks in her mouth!

She could see them all in the dock of the District Court, with her mother crying and Sourpuss in the Witness Box telling the DJ what they had done. What excuse could they possibly give for it?

'You needn't pretend it's all our fault,' said Whacker. 'The ould man told us how yous tormented him.'

The Dancer spread his hands in a graceful movement that had just the suggestion of a shrug.

'Medical treatment is not always comfortable,' he said. 'Mr. Mooney has a horror of injections, and his mind has been far from clear lately. You would be very foolish to pay too much heed to an old man's hallucinations.'

For a moment, even Richie was shaken. Then he remembered the Will. 'What about this then?' He waved the Will defiantly at the Dancer. 'You're no doctor, you're just after this! But you're not getting it!'

'No, wait, Richie,' Linda said. 'If grandfather's alive I must think what's best for him.'

'*If* he's still alive,' said Richie.

'Linda can see for herself,' replied the Dancer.

'You mean trickster!' cried Maura, to her own surprise. 'Don't you know well Linda can't see!'

'A slip of the tongue,' said the Dancer smoothly. 'If she promises to behave herself I'll allow her to go up to the old man's room. I've been at his bedside for the past half-hour.' He smiled again. 'That's why you didn't see me when you started your tricks with Mrs. Coffey. The old man is breathing loud enough for anyone to hear.'

'I must go to him,' Linda said.

Whacker grabbed her by the sleeve. 'And maybe find yerself locked in yer room again?' he said. 'It could easy be a trick. We'll all go.'

'Very well,' agreed the Dancer, 'provided you all behave yourselves. But I want you first to promise that if you find what I've said is true you'll hand over that piece of paper you have and stay away from this house in future.'

'I'm promisin' nothing,' said Richie. 'You can't stop us goin' upstairs if we want. You can't stop us doin' anything.'

'There's just one small thing you've overlooked,' said the Dancer, and his voice was so gentle that it was almost tender. 'Whether the old man lives or dies depends on me. Even if he lives, you know, he could live for weeks in terrible pain unless I take care of him.'

'No!' screamed Linda.

'He's only foolin' you, Linda,' said Whacker. 'He's not a doctor. And we'll make sure he can't harm your grand-da anymore!'

But Linda shook her head. 'If grand-dad's all

right that's all that matters,' she said. 'I don't care about the Will. Give it to him, Richie!'

'Not till I've seen the ould man,' said Richie.

'Will you promise to give it to me when you do?' asked the Dancer.

'Please, Richie!' cried Linda. 'Please do!'

Richie looked defeated. He was sure they were making a dreadful mistake, but how could he go against Linda and the longing in her voice? He suddenly realized what it must be like for her, with her father and mother dead and the old man upstairs the only one of her family left.

'If the ould man is really still alive, I will,' he said.

Whacker gave him such a look of disappointment that Richie knew he felt that he had let him down. The Dancer smiled. It was the smile of a man who had victory in his grasp.

'Then come on up and take a look at him,' he said. 'But you must all keep very quiet. His life may depend on it.'

He turned and led the way upstairs. Richie and Whacker both watched him closely in case he might try any tricks. Suddenly Linda darted ahead, as sure-footed as if she had the full use of her two eyes.

May brought up the rear of the party. Unlike Richie, Whacker and Maura, she had never been upstairs before and she looked around her in curiosity. As the others surged through the door at the top of the stairs, she noticed the key was still in the lock, a bunch of other keys hanging from it by a large ring. On impulse, she pulled it from the lock and pushed the whole bunch into her pocket. That way, she thought, no trick of the Dancer could end up with Linda being locked into her room again.

Inside the room, the old man lay just as Richie and Whacker had last seen him. For a moment, Richie was sure the Dancer was trying to fool them again, for the face on the pillow was like ivory. They all hung back instinctively, awed by the feeling of death that hung over the room — all, that is, except Linda. Unable to see the sunken face that so chilled the others, she was only conscious of the sound of shallow breathing that came from the old man's body.

'Grand-dad!' she cried, running forward. 'Grand-dad! You're not dead after all!'

'You see!' The Dancer turned to Richie. 'Perhaps in future you won't be in such a hurry to interfere! Now will you please give me that piece of paper?'

Richie looked desperately at Linda, but she was already kneeling by the bedside. She had no interest in the Will anymore, he thought. She cares only about her grandfather. Reluctantly he handed the Will to the Dancer, who thrust it inside his jacket, smiling triumphantly. Only then did he seem to become aware of what Linda was doing.

'Leave him alone!' he ordered angrily, trying too late to intercept her. 'D'you want to kill him? A sudden shock could be fatal!'

But Linda already had the old man in her arms,

her cheek against his. It is doubtful if she even heard the Dancer's words.

'It's all right, grand-dad!' she whispered softly. 'It's Linda. There's nothing to be afraid of now!'

'He can't hear you, you little fool! He's in a coma!' snapped the Dancer, his usual calm shattered as he tried to pull Linda away from the bed.

'You can wake up now, grand-dad!' continued Linda, as if she could not even feel the Dancer tugging angrily at her arm. And then a surprising thing happened.

There was a sudden change in the old man's breathing and his eyes slowly opened. He looked at Linda and smiled — and the smile brought a flicker of life to the death-like features.

'Linda,' he said in a weak, shaky voice, 'Linda, promise you won't tell.'

Linda went very white, but when she spoke May thought that her voice had the same calm, reassuring tone that her mother always used to her baby brother when he was hurt or frightened.

'It doesn't matter about all that now, grand-dad,' she said, 'because now you're going to live. My friends are here to make sure they don't kill you. If they destroy that Will all you have to do is to write another.'

Out of the corner of his eye, Richie saw the Dancer's face contort with rage. With arms outstretched, he suddenly flung himself on to the bed, his hands reaching for the old man's throat.

8 *And Tickly under There*

As the Dancer moved, so did Richie, catching the man in a kind of rugby tackle that sent them both rolling across the floor. The Dancer struggled with him but the others were upon him now, forcing him face downwards on the floor. Then Richie and Whacker sat on him.

'What's going on?' asked Linda fearfully.

'Just taking care of a certain party known to many as Dancer,' said Richie grinning.

'You can take the Will back from him now,' said Imelda.

'Better leave it where it is,' said May. 'The Guards'll believe our story better if they find it in the Dancer's pocket.'

'The Guards?' echoed Maura fearfully.

May nodded. 'We'll have to tell them now,' she said. 'Now we know we were right about Sourpuss and the Dancer.'

Suddenly the old man sighed, causing Linda to run her hands anxiously over his face. 'Are you all right, grand-dad ?' she asked.

When the old man spoke his voice was so weak that they could hardly hear him, but there was no doubt that he was smiling.

'Yes, I'm fine, thanks to your young friends here.'

'All the same,' Linda said. 'I think we'd better get you your old doctor back!'

'Dr. Meath,' said the old man with an effort. 'You'll find his name in the book beside the 'phone downstairs.' Then his eyelids flickered and closed as if the effort of speaking had been too much for him.

'Better do as he says,' Whacker said, 'and you can ring the Guards at the same time. Richie and me'll take care of the Dancer.'

Mickser and the three girls ran down to the 'phone, but there was no address book beside it. Mickser pulled open the drawer in the table but it was not there either.

'Sourpuss musta moved it,' May said.

'Next door,' cried Maura suddenly. 'The woman next door. Come on!' She ran out of the front door and down the path to the gate with the others after her.

The housekeeper opened the door, surprised at their frantic knocking, but before she could even ask what was wrong, Maura grabbed her arm.

'Would you know how we could get hold of Dr. Meath?' she asked 'Linda's grand-da's real bad and we can't find the book with his number in it. That Dancer is no doctor at all, only after the grand-da's Will.'

'Didn't I know there was something wrong there?' said the old lady. 'Come on in, all of you and I'll get Dr. Meath's number for you.'

'Maybe you'd ring him for us?' asked May, as they

86

followed her into the hall. 'He might take more notice of you.'

'I'll be glad to,' said the old woman. 'I never did like that Mrs. Coffey, ever since she ran poor Lizzie,' and she dialled a number as the others sat on the stairs and waited.

'Dr. Meath?' they heard the old woman say. 'I'm ringing for old Mr. Mooney next door . . .' but before she had time to say any more they suddenly heard loud shouting from outside. They ran out into the garden.

They could hear Richie's voice from the far side of the wall and, as they reached the gate, they saw the Dancer pulling Mrs. Coffey out on to the road. From one wrist May's piece of twine still hung.

'After them!' shouted May, as the Dancer and Mrs. Coffey started to run towards the railway bridge. At that moment, Richie and Whacker hurtled out of the gate in pursuit and cannoned into May and Imelda knocking them all off balance. By the time they had recovered the Dancer and Mrs. Coffey had had a good start. Maura realized that once they reached Phibsboro' it would be impossible to catch them.

'They're getting away on us,' she cried desperately, but even at that moment the two hurrying figures ahead of them turned abruptly off to the right on to the railway embankment.

'Why are they going that way?' gasped May. Then the sight of a squad car crossing the bridge gave them the answer. For a moment they hoped the Guards might intercept their quarry but the car, ignoring both groups of hurrying figures, passed slowly on down the North Circular Road.

'The bikes,' gasped Whacker suddenly. 'If they find our bikes they'll get away on them!' He flung himself on to the embankment wall, just in time to hear a sharp cry from the darkness below.

Two figures were stretched out beneath them in a tangled heap. Not expecting or seeing the bikes in the dark shadow cast by the railway bridge, the Dancer and Mrs. Coffey had tripped over them and rolled down the side of the embankment. Before they could pick themselves up, the six pursuers were on top of them, pinning them down.

'Got ya!' cried Whacker triumphantly, 'and this time you won't get away from us!'

But Maura, sprawled across Mrs. Coffey's legs, felt less confident. 'But what are we gonna do with them?' she asked. 'We can't sit here for ever?'

'We can use the bit of twine to tie their hands together,' Richie said. 'Then we can move without letting them go.'

So while Whacker and Richie held the Dancer, and Mickser and Maura pinned down the protesting Mrs. Coffey, May and Imelda tied the Dancer's hands together behind his back with the piece of twine still hanging from Mrs. Coffey's wrist. Then they helped them cautiously to their feet.

The fact that they were tied together made it

harder for them to escape, but it did not make it easier to get them up the side of the embankment. And from the way the Dancer's eyes flicked here and there he was obviously looking for a way to escape again.

'What are we gonna do with them?' Maura asked. 'We can't take them down the North Circular Road like that.'

'Have to,' said Richie shortly, but secretly he had been thinking the same thing.

Suddenly the Dancer's feet seemed to go from under him and he was on the ground, dragging Mrs. Coffey down with him. Bending over him in the growing darkness, Whacker saw that there was a rusty piece of metal lying on the bank beside him, the remains of a broken down car that someone had flung down the side of the cutting, and the Dancer was frantically working the twine that bound him across the jagged edge of metal.

'Stop that,' he yelled but, before he could prevent it, the frayed piece of twine snapped and the Dancer was off like a hare along the side of the cutting.

'After him,' shouted Whacker, as he and Richie took off in pursuit, but it was too late. The Dancer had disappeared into the shelter of the bushes that fringed the cutting and the sound of his body crashing through shrubbery echoed back from above.

'He'll have reached the road by now!' said Maura hopelessly, as she and May clung to Mrs. Coffey to stop her following the Dancer. 'They'll never catch him now.'

'You might as well be trying to tie up an eel,' said May, 'but at least we've still got Sourpuss. Come on. Let's get her outa this.'

All the same, it was a dishevelled and depressed little group that struggled out on to the road with Mrs. Coffey held firmly between them. Then, however, they got a surprise. Richie and Whacker were standing beside a squad car while two Guards were pushing the Dancer into the back of the car.

'Bring Sourpuss over here,' called Richie and, though Mrs. Coffey struggled at the sight of the Guards, she was soon seated in the back of the car beside the Dancer.

'I don't understand. Where did the bluebottles come from?' asked Maura.

'The woman next door rang them after she spoke to Dr. Meath,' Richie told her, 'and the Dancer ran straight into their arms.'

But none of them really understood everything that had happened until a week later when Linda's grandfather came out of hospital. Linda had not been on her own all that time, of course. The doctor and the housekeeper between them had managed to find Lizzie, who had needed very little persuading to come back. When the old man was settled in his home once more Linda decided to give a home-coming party in his honour.

'There'll only be ourselves,' she said, 'because grand-dad tires easily and he won't want a lot of noise, but he wants to meet you all again, so will you come on Sunday about four o'clock?'

So on Sunday the six from the Square scrubbed their nails and put on their best clothes and set out for the North Circular Road. This time they brought Patchie with them, running beside the bikes, because there was not so much traffic across town on a Sunday and Linda wanted to meet him.

There were ham sandwiches for tea, and egg and tomato sandwiches, and jelly and trifle and chocolate cake and eclairs and jam rolls and every sort of biscuit. Linda kept slipping biscuits to Patchie who thought it must be his birthday. Then, when even Whacker agreed that he could not manage another mouthful, Linda's grandfather said it was time to talk.

'I want to thank you,' he said, 'because without you I wouldn't be alive today!'

'Ah, now, I don't know about that ...' began Richie, but the old man held up a hand to silence him.

'There's a lot you still don't know,' he said. 'You see, that evil cousin of mine had been mixing something in with my food — that was why she had to get rid of Lizzie there.'

'You mean, she was poisoning you?' asked Whacker incredulously, feeling that he had somehow got himself into one of the detective series he was so fond of watching on the telly.

The old man nodded.

'Very, very slowly,' he said. 'They didn't want to kill me, d'you see, until they had the Will, but they wanted everyone to know I was sick so no one would be surprised when I suddenly died. The plan was to finish me off as soon as they had destroyed the Will, but they couldn't find it. I'd hidden it, d'you see, knowing there were so many robbers in the town.'

'But why did they want to destroy the Will?' asked May. 'Was there another one, like Linda thought?'

'There was indeed,' the old man said, 'and my cousin had a copy of it, but it was no use to her once there was a later one. Of course, my solicitor had a copy of the later one, but he died three months ago. His affairs had reached a chaotic state towards the end. A lot of things couldn't be found and my Will was amongst them. Also, he had talked too much about things he shouldn't. That's how my cousin came to hear that I'd changed my Will and that I had the only copy of it.'

'And she came here to steal it and murder you?' gasped May. Bad and all as Mrs. Coffey was, she never thought she would go as far as that.

'I don't think so,' the old man said. 'I think she just hoped that if she came here and fussed around me and looked after me I'd change my Will again, but you see I'd got very fond of this young one here in the meantime,' and he put an arm around Linda, who planted a kiss on the top of his head.

92

'And when you wouldn't change it she got the idea of stealin' it,' mused Whacker, but the old man shook his head.

'I wouldn't say now that it was her idea,' he said, 'but that monster she brought into the house.'

'You mean, the Dancer?' asked Maura.

'I don't know what he does for a living,' the old man replied, 'but he's as evil a man as ever I hope to meet. Is he a dancer?'

'Ah, no,' said Maura. 'I dunno what he does. We just call him that because of the way he moves.'

The grandfather nodded.

'More like a cat I'd have said,' he commented, 'but I see what you mean. Though who he is and where he came from I don't know.'

'He was gonna marry Sourpuss,' May told him.

'She means Mrs. Coffey,' Linda explained, as her grandfather raised his eyebrows.

'I see,' said the old man. 'So that explains it.'

'But not if she was a pauper,' May added. 'I heard him say so when I was weeding the cabbage patch next door.'

At that the old man laughed.

'I wouldn't exactly describe her as a pauper,' he said, 'but maybe your Dancer has expensive tastes. I doubt if he'll be able to indulge them much for the next few years though.

'Will he go to gaol?' asked Mickser.

'I imagine so,' Mr. Mooney said. 'The Guards seem to think they have a fairly strong case. They came to see me while I was in hospital.'

Then Maura asked what she had been wondering for the past two weeks.

'Why did the Guards believe our story so easy?'

Mr. Mooney laughed. 'The first thing the doctor did when he got me to hospital was to pump out my stomach,' he said, 'and have the contents analysed. I suppose he must have thought I showed the symptoms of poisoning as soon as he saw me. Anyway, he asked me who had been bringing me my food. He must have rung the Guards and alerted them.'

'So that's the why,' said Maura. 'And did they give you back the Will they took offa the Dancer?'

Mr. Mooney shook his head. 'I think they want that for evidence,' he said.

'So you'll have to make another one after all,' said Imelda.

The old man laughed.

'I daresay they'll give it back to me when they're finished with it,' he said, 'but I was thinking of making a new one anyway. I'd left a small sum to my cousin and I certainly won't do that now. Also, you see, it occurred to me while I was in hospital that Linda might have been left all alone in the house if I had died. I was thinking that, as well as having Lizzie in the house, Linda ought to have a companion.'

'I don't need a companion,' said Linda. 'I'd just like to have Maura here for company.'

'That's what a companion means,' her

grandfather told her. 'If Maura were free she would be just the sort of person I had in mind.'

'I wish I could do it,' said Maura, 'but I have to work because my father's on the Labour.'

The old man smiled. 'That's what I meant about changing my Will,' he said. 'There'd be money provided to deal with that.'

'Oh, but I couldn't take money,' said Maura. 'That wouldn't be right. Not unless I worked for it.'

'But you would,' said the old man. 'It would be a job like any other job. I'm happy to say there's no need for a permanent companion while I'm still alive. I may be poor company for a young girl but Linda seems happy enough. However, if you get tired of the gardening and want a job for the holidays, I'm sure Lizzie could always use an extra pair of hands around the house.'

At that everyone cheered and Patchie joined in the general excitement with his shrill bark. Linda started to laugh and the more Patchie barked the more she laughed.

'What's so funny?' demanded May, almost hurt that Patchie should be looked on as a figure of fun.

Linda could hardly speak for laughing, but when she finally managed to control herself, she gasped:

'It's ridiculous, I know, but Patchie barks just like Whacker!' and when they had all finished laughing they had to agree that it was absolutely true.

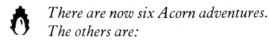 *There are now six Acorn adventures.*
The others are:

Robbers in the House *Carolyn Swift*

In the heart of old Dublin, six children discover a thrilling new place to play. But they meet two suspicious-looking characters, combing the place with what looks like a vacuum cleaner. Is there buried treasure?

Robbers in the Hills *Carolyn Swift*

Another adventure for the Square children as they explore the Dublin mountains. But why does their farmer friend turn on them and drive them away? What is the mystery?

The Big Push *Joe O'Donnell*

A teen-age group is pushing a brass bed from Dublin to Wexford for the National Rock Finals. Why are so many people interested in that bed. How far will they go to get it?

The Legend of the Golden Key
Tom McCaughren

The legend of this book was born in County Antrim in the days of the 1798 Rebellion. The setting is an ancient castle. There are ghosts, phantoms, fairy gold and star-crossed lovers ...

The Legend of the Phantom Highwayman *Tom McCaughren*

Is it true that the highwayman Hugh Rua rides again? Has it any connection with the smuggling of the 'quare stuff' from down the mountains? Tapser and his friends decide to unravel the secret of the glen.